Watch Me!

Margaret Mahy is a New Zealander and has loved thinking up stories ever since she was a small girl. She has been awarded the highly acclaimed Carnegie Medal twice (for *The Haunting* - published in 1982, and *The Changeover* - 1984) and the Esther Glen Award six times. She lives near Christchurch, South Island in a house she partially built herself. Margaret has two grown-up daughters, six grandchildren, two cats and a standard poodle called Boozer.

Also by Margaret Mahy

Wonderful Me!
Wait for Me!

Watch Me!

Margaret Mahy

Illustrated by Peter Bailey

Dolphin Paperbacks

First published in this edition in 2004 by
Dolphin Paperbacks
a division of the Orion Publishing Group Ltd
Orion House
5 Upper St Martin's Lane
London WC2H 9EA

First published by J M Dent & Sons Ltd in 1973
as *The Third Margaret Mahy Storybook*

Typeset at The Spartan Press Ltd,
Lymington, Hants

Printed in Great Britain by
Clays Ltd, St Ives plc

A catalogue record for this book is
available from the British Library.

ISBN 1 84255 093 4

www.orionbooks.co.uk

Contents

Aunt Nasty

'Oh dear!' said Mother, one lunch time, after she had read a letter the postman had just left.

'What's the matter?' asked Father. Even Toby and Claire looked up from their boiled eggs.

'Aunt Nasty has written to say she is coming to stay with us,' said Mother. 'The thought of it makes me worried.'

'You must tell her we will be out!' cried Toby. He did not like the sound of Aunt Nasty.

'Or say we have no room,' said Father.

'You know I can't do that,' said Mother. 'Remember Aunt Nasty is a *witch*.'

Toby and Claire looked at each other with round eyes. They had forgotten, for a moment, that Aunt Nasty was a witch as well as being an aunt. If they said there was no room in the house Aunt Nasty might be very cross. She might turn them into frogs.

'She is coming on the Viscount tomorrow,' said Mother, looking at the letter. 'It is hard to read this witch-writing. She writes it with a magpie's feather and all the letters look like broomsticks.'

'I see she has written it on mouse skin,' said Father.

'Isn't she just showing off?' asked Toby. 'If she was a real witch she would ride a broomstick here . . . not come on the Viscount.'

Claire had to move into Toby's room so that Aunt Nasty would have a bedroom all to herself. She put a vase of flowers in the room, but they were not garden flowers. Aunt Nasty liked flowers of a poisonous kind, like woody nightshade and foxgloves.

'Leave the cobwebs in that corner,' said Father. 'Remember how cross she was when you swept them down last time. She loves dust and cobwebs. All witches do.'

The next afternoon they went to the airport to meet Aunt Nasty. It was easy to see her in the crowd getting off the Viscount. She was one of the old sort of witch, all in black with a pointed hat and a broomstick.

'Hello, Aunt Nasty,' said Mother. 'How nice to see you again.'

'I don't suppose you are really pleased to see me,' said Aunt Nasty, 'but that doesn't matter. There is a special meeting of witches in the city this week. That is why I had to come. I will be out every night on my broom, and trying to sleep during the day. I hope the children are quiet.'

'Why didn't you come on your broom, Aunt Nasty?' asked Toby. 'Why did you have to come in the aeroplane?'

'Don't you ever listen to the weather report on the radio?' said Aunt Nasty crossly. 'It said there would be fresh winds in the Cook Strait area, increasing to gale force at midday. It isn't much fun riding a broomstick in a fresh wind let me tell you. Even the silly aeroplane bucked around. I began to think they'd put us into a wheelbarrow by mistake. Two people were sick.'

'Poor people,' said Claire.

'Serve them right!' Aunt Nasty muttered. 'People with weak stomachs annoy me.'

When they got home Aunt Nasty went straight to her room. She smiled at the sight of the foxgloves and the woody nightshade, but she did not say thank you.

'I will have a catnap,' she said, stroking the raggy black fur collar she wore. 'I hope the bed is not damp or lumpy. I used to enjoy a damp bed when I was a young witch, but I'm getting old now.'

Then she shut the door. They heard her put her suitcase against it.

'What a rude aunt!' said Toby.

'She has to be rude, because of being a witch,' said Mother. 'Now, do be nice quiet children, won't you! Don't make her cross or she might turn you into tad-poles.'

The children went out to play, but they were not happy.

'I don't like Aunt Nasty,' said Claire.

'I don't like having a witch in the house,' said Toby.

The house was very very quiet and strange while Aunt Nasty was there. Everyone spoke in whispery voices and went around on tiptoe. Aunt Nasty stayed in her room most of the time. Once she came out of her room and asked for some

toadstools. Toby found some for her under
a pine tree at the top of the hill . . . fine red
ones with spots, but Aunt Nasty was not
pleased with them.

'These are dreadful toadstools,' she said.
'They look good but they are quite
disappointing. The brown, slimy ones
are much better. You can't trust a boy
to do anything properly these days. But

I suppose I will have to make do with them.'

That was on Tuesday. Some smoke came out of the keyhole on Wednesday, and on Thursday Aunt Nasty broke a soup plate. However, they did not see her again until Friday. Then she came out and complained that there was not enough pepper in the soup.

At last it was Sunday. Aunt Nasty had been there a week. Now she was going home again – this time by broomstick. Toby and Claire were very pleased. Mother was pleased too, and yet she looked tired and sad. She went out to take some plants to the woman next door. While she was out Father came in from the garden suddenly.

'Do you know what?' he said to Toby and Claire. 'I have just remembered something. It is your mother's birthday today and we have forgotten all about it.

7

That is what comes of having a witch in the house. We must go and buy birthday presents at once.'

'But it's Sunday, Daddy!' cried Claire. 'All the shops will be shut!'

'What on earth shall we do?' asked Father. 'There must be some way of getting a present for her.'

'A present!' said a voice. 'Who wants a present?' It was Aunt Nasty with her suitcase, a broomstick and a big black cat at her heels.

'Oh, look at the cat!' cried Claire. 'I did not know you had a cat, Aunt Nasty.'

'He sits round my neck when we ride in the bus or the plane,' said Aunt Nasty proudly. 'It is his own idea, and it is a good one, because people think he is a fur collar and I do not have to buy a ticket for him. But what is this I hear? Have you really forgotten to get your mother a birthday present?'

'I'm afraid we have!' said Father sadly.

'Ha!' said Aunt Nasty fiercely. 'Now I never ever forgot my mother's birthday. I always had some little gift for her. Once I gave her the biggest blackest rat you ever saw. It was fine rat and I would have liked it for my own pet, but nothing was too good for my mother. I let her have it.'

'I don't think Mummy would like a rat,' said Claire.

'I wasn't going to give her one!' snapped Aunt Nasty. 'Tell me, can you children draw?'

'Yes,' said Toby and Claire.

'Can you draw a birthday cake, jellies, little cakes, sandwiches, roast chickens, bottles of fizzy lemonade, balloons, crackers, pretty flowers, birds and butterflies . . . and presents too?'

'Yes!' said Toby and Claire.

'Well then, you draw them,' said Aunt Nasty, 'And I will cook up some magic.

Where is the oven? Hmmm! I see it is an electric stove. It is a bit on the clean side, isn't it? An old black stove is of much more use to a witch. Mind you I've got no use for the witch who can't make do with what she can get. I will work something out, you see if I don't.'

Claire drew and Toby drew. They covered lots and lots of pages with drawings of cakes and balloons and presents wrapped in pretty paper.

Aunt Nasty came in with a smoking saucepan. 'Give me your drawings,' she said. 'Hurry up, I haven't got all day. Hmmmm! They aren't very good, are they? But they'll have to do. A good witch can manage with a scribble if she has to.'

She popped the drawings into the saucepan where they immediately caught fire and burned up to ashes. A thick blue smoke filled the room. No one could see anyone else.

'This smoke tastes like birthday cake,'
called Claire.

'It tastes like jelly and ice-cream,' said
Toby. The smoke began to go away up the
chimney.

'I smell flowers,' said Father.

Then they saw that the whole room was
changed.

Everywhere there were leaves and
flowers and birds only as big as your little
fingernail. The table was covered with
jellies of all colours, and little cakes and
sandwiches. There was a trifle and two
roast chickens. There were huge wooden
dishes of fruit - even grapes, cherries and
pineapples. There was a big silver bowl of
fizzy lemonade with rose petals floating
in it. All around the table were presents
and crackers and balloons - so many of
them they would have come up to your
knees.

'Aha!' said Aunt Nasty, looking pleased. 'I

haven't lost my touch with a bit of pretty magic.'

Best of all was the birthday cake. It was so big there was no room for it on the table.

It stood like a pink and white mountain by the fireplace. The balloons bounced and floated around the room. The tiny birds flew everywhere singing. One of them made a nest as small as a thimble in a vase of flowers.

'What is in this parcel?' asked Claire, pointing to a parcel that moved and rustled. 'Is it a rat?'

'It's two pigeons,' said Aunt Nasty. 'There is a pigeon house for them in one of the other parcels. Well, I must be off. I've wasted enough time. The saucepan is spoilt by the way, but you won't mind that. It was a nasty cheap one anyhow.'

'Won't you stay and wish Mummy a happy birthday?' asked Toby. 'She would like to say thank you for her birthday party.'

'Certainly not!' said Aunt Nasty. 'I never ever say thank you myself. I don't expect anyone to say it to me. I love rudeness, but that is because I am a witch. You are not witches, so make sure you are polite to everybody.' She tied her suitcase to her broomstick with string and her cat climbed onto her shoulder.

'Goodbye to you anyway,' she said. 'I don't like children, but you are better than most. Perhaps I will see you again or perhaps I won't.' She got on her broomstick and flew out of the window, her suitcase bobbing behind her. She was a bit wobbly.

'Well,' said Father, 'she wasn't so bad after all. It will be strange not having a witch in the house any more.'

'Mother will love her birthday,' said Claire. 'It was good of Aunt Nasty. It is the prettiest party I have ever seen.'

'I don't even mind if she visits us again next year,' said Toby.

'Look, there is Mummy coming now,' said Father. 'Let's go and meet her.'

They all ran out into the sunshine shouting 'Happy Birthday!' Toby had a quick look up in the air for Aunt Nasty. There far above him he saw a tiny little black speck that might have been Aunt Nasty or it might have been a seagull. He

was not quite sure. Then he took one of
Mother's hands, and Claire took the other,
and they pulled her, laughing and happy,
up the steps into her birthday room.

The Green Fair

Look, children, look at the fair.

It has come in the night. It is there.

Like a flock of bright birds the tents have settled, spreading their wings in the morning wind.

There are two merry-go-rounds waiting. There is popcorn, candy floss, fizzy lemonade and ice cream. There are tents with wonderful things inside them – ghost trains, mermaids, merry monkeys, clever mice that can dance a jig and play on drums no bigger than walnuts.

The farmers have brought all their animals to win prizes – horses stamp, cows

moo. The sheep blink sadly at each other.
The pigs snuffle and sleep.

The fair is waiting to begin. All over town
people open doors. The children spill
outside, laughing and shouting in the clear
morning sunlight.

On the edge of the fair is a little brown
tent; it is like a pine cone in the grass.

Who is it sitting outside the little tent? His
thin hands on his knees are like rustly
brown leaves curled around each other.

At the doorways of the other bright tents
men shout and dance and call people in.
This man does not smile or shout. He is as
still as a man carved of wood.

Only the magpies and the sparrows come
to his tent and he lets them inside. What is
inside the brown tent, the pine-cone tent
small and still on the edge of the noisy
fair?

Two big boys come by. They have jingly
money in their pockets.

'What's in this tent?' they ask the man outside.

'The Green Fair,' says the man, and he looks at them with narrow green eyes, like blades of grass.

The Green Fair? What is the Green Fair?

'How much does it cost to go inside?' the boys ask.

'It costs 50p to go inside.'

'It is the cheapest tent in the whole show.'

'It is too cheap and small to be any good,' the boys say to each other. 'We will have another ride on the merry-go-round.'

Off they go, jingling their pockets.

'The Green Fair?' says a woodmouse who is listening. 'What is the Green Fair?'

'It is free to mice,' says the man. The mouse scurries into the little brown tent, the pine-cone tent, on the edge of the fair.

Then a lot of little children come by. The oldest is seven and the smallest is three.

They have no money. They are looking for bottles to sell.

'What is in this tent?' they ask the man.

'The Green Fair,' he says. He smiles for the first time.

'Why don't you stamp and shout? Why don't you call people in?' asks a little girl.

'I don't need to,' says the man. 'The right people come to me. It costs 50p to go in.'

'We don't even have 50p,' says a boy.

'What is that by your foot?' asks the man. There by the boy's foot a 50p lies in the grass. Perhaps one of the big boys dropped it.

'We can buy popcorn now,' cried a child. But no – all the children want to go into the little brown pine-cone tent. They all want to see the Green Fair.

'Everybody can go in for 50p,' says the man. 'Here are your tickets.'

What is this? He gathers a handful of

grass. Each child takes a blade of grass and goes into the little brown tent. It is so small they have to get down on their knees to go in.

Inside the tent . . . what is inside the tent?

A forest of tall trees.

Perhaps it is the oldest forest of all. Perhaps it has been growing there since the first morning. Moss has spread out over the trunks and branches.

How can an old old forest be growing in a little brown tent?

How can the trees be so tall and stretch so wide?

'Is is magic?' asks a child.

'Magic,' says an echo, as if the forest was answering, but really the forest is still, so still you can hear the spiders spin their cobwebs. The children think it must be magic. The forest feels magical – it is quiet waiting for something to happen.

Under the trees is a merry-go-round. Its horses swing on ropes plaited of rushes and its roof is covered with ferns and moss.

Perhaps it is the oldest merry-go-round in the world.

Perhaps someone planted a seed there – a merry-go-round seed – which grew into a merry-go-round.

There are just enough horses for the children to have one each. They scramble on, the horses begin to toss their heads and kick up their heels. Slowly they begin their dance round and round in the green light of the forest.

Look – the forest comes alive. Out from under the ferns come little animals carrying wooden dishes of fruit – the plum, the pear, the apple, and grapes both white and purple. Someone begins to play on a penny recorder.

The Green Fair has begun.

Now the furry people put up small green stalls. They smile all over their whiskery faces and beckon the children to come and see. Everything in the Green Fair is free. You can win prizes too.

You can win – a nest of singing birds,
a bear carved out of a
cherry stone,
a doll tiny enough to live
in a matchbox,

a tiger skin with fierce
eyes and white teeth,
a pair of dancing shoes
sewn all over with
flowers,
a cricket in a cage of
willow.

Every child wins a prize, even the smallest
child of all. She wins a little wooden box.
When she opens the box a frog plays a tune
on a green violin. She must remember to
give the frog brown bread soaked in milk,
or he will hop away. Yes, he will hop away
and take his green violin with him.

All the time the merry-go-round goes
round and round, round and round, under
the green leaves.

The bush rats come out from the mossy
hollows. They are the music-makers. They
play on the drum, the flute, the bells and
the tinkle-tankle harp.

The children can listen and laugh, they

can dance and sing. They don't need to
know any words. They can make them
up.

'Oh, the Green Fair!
Oh, the Green Fair!
And everyone happy under the leaves.'

Now the feasting begins.
Out come dishes of nuts,
    plates of little cakes,
    shivery jellies coloured like rainbows,
    leaves filled with blackberries,
    flowers filled with strawberries,
    honey from a wild bee's nest, dripping
        golden from the honeycomb.
There is a fire. You can sizzle sausages if
you want to. You wrap them in a slice of
fresh brown bread and eat them hot, hot,
hot. They are burnt on the outside, but that
is all the better.

There is fizzy lemonade. As you open the

bottle it sings its song to you. There is grape juice and apple juice and slices of orange.

This is the feast of the Green Fair.

But the merry-go-round spins slower and slower. At last it stops. It is time to go. The Green Fair is over. The furry people fold up their stalls. The forest goes still again . . . so still you can hear the spiders spin their webs.

The children must go now, but they are happy, sticky children. (This is how children are when they have visited the Green Fair.) They hold their prizes tightly. They will keep them for ever. Their pockets are filled with the cakes and nuts they cannot eat. They whistle and sing and shout as they tumble home.

'Did you have a good time?' asks the mother of the littlest girl.

The littlest girl opens her wooden box. Up jumps the frog and plays a tune on his green violin.

'I must remember to give him bread and milk,' she says, 'and then he will stay for ever.'

'Ah,' says her mother, 'you have been to the Green Fair. I went once when I was little like you. I won a musical box, small as a bird's egg. I still have it in my box of treasures. It plays the songs of the Green Fair.'

Late at night the big, bright fair is dark and still. The moon comes up. It sees a lonely light on the edge of the big fair. There sits the man beside his little brown tent.

His thin hands are like rustly brown leaves curled around each other. His narrow eyes shine like blades of grass in the moonlight. He lets the mice, the bush bats, the owls, the moths and the people of the night go into his tent.

They all want to visit the Green Fair.

As he sits there he remembers the littlest

girl. He thinks of a long time ago, and remembers her mother. He remembers back to the oldest time of all when the old forest was planted and the Green Fair began to grow.

'The right people always find me,' he thinks and he smiles.

The Storm
King's Daughter

A young man stood by the edge of a stream,
And the Storm King's daughter saw him
  there,
And down she whirled like a wild witch
  dream
Wrapped all around in her long black hair.

'Carry me, carry me over the water!'
'Who are you, who are you?'
'I'm the Storm's daughter.
The river rises under my hand
Running in ruin over the land.

Even the ocean, breaking free
From moon-mapped courses, follows me,
While over the hills my father cries
Shaking the summits, bruising the skies.
Around his neck on coppery rings
Are dragons' jewels and crowns of kings.
Carry me, carry me over the water,'
Cried the Storm King's strange and beautiful
    daughter.

'I'll not carry you over the water
For you can flow from here to there,
Or ride on the wind, or swim like a swan,
Or weave a bridge from your long black
    hair.'

But the Storm King's daughter took the
    young man
Between finger and thumb like a wheaten
    grain
And carried him off to her castle of thunder,
Drawing behind her a curtain of rain.

The Breakfast Bird

'Look!' said Johnny, 'Look at Cathie's toast!'

Everyone looked at Cathie's toast.

'Oh, Cathie!' said their mother. 'You've done it again. There is honey everywhere.'

There was honey all over Cathie's toast.

There was honey all over Cathie's plate.

There was honey all over Cathie's face.

'You have even got it on the tablecloth,' said their mother.

'Well, I like honey,' said Cathie. 'I like *plenty* of honey.'

'You are a greedy honey bear,' said their mother. 'Most of that honey will be wasted.'

'Not if I lick my plate out in the kitchen,' replied Cathie. 'It won't be wasted then.'

'Bad manners though!' said Mack, the eldest of the children.

'It isn't bad manners out in the kitchen,' argued Johnny. 'Licking plates is only bad manners at the table.'

This was a family rule.

'As long as she doesn't try to lick the tablecloth,' Mack answered in a grunty voice. Things began to quieten down. Then Johnny began again.

'Mum, you know Mr Cooney's budgie has hatched out babies.'

'No, how should I know?' said Johnny's mother. 'You've only told me twenty times already.' She was trying to scrape honey off the tablecloth as she spoke.

'Well, can't I have one? Please, *please*!' begged Johnny. 'I'd teach it to talk and perch on my finger. Mr Cooney's budgie perches on his finger.'

'Yes, you might teach it to perch,' said his mother, 'but would you remember to give it fresh water? Would you clean out its cage and make sure it had plenty of seed every day? I don't think you would.'

'Yes, I would!' Johnny cried quickly, his eyes blue and startled in his freckled face. 'I'd help in the garden too. Budgies like something fresh and green every day.'

Johnny's mother laughed.

'I'll tell you what . . .' she said at last. 'Today, Cathie's Play Centre group finishes for the holidays. The mothers have to take the pets home and feed them and look after them until the Play Centre begins again. Shall I bring the budgie home? Then we can see just how good you are at looking after a budgie.'

'He's a nice budgie,' called Cathie. 'His name is Nippy because he tries to bite our fingers.'

'If he bit your finger,' said Mack, 'he'd get a

beakful of honey. His beak would be all stuck up for hours.'

When Johnny came home from school the next day his mother said, 'There's a visitor in the sitting-room.'

'Yes,' Cathie cried like a squeaky echo, 'there's a green visitor sitting on the table.'

The green visitor was Nippy, the Play Centre budgie.

Johnny wanted a blue budgie, not a green one.

He went up to the Play Centre cage and looked at Nippy.

Nippy looked back at Johnny from little black eyes. Nippy looked like a small round-shouldered pirate. He looked like a goblin in a green shawl. He shuffled along his perch, six steps left, six steps right. Then he hooked his beak over the wire of the cage, crawled up the wire and hung upside-down on the roof.

'Will he sit on my finger?' asked Johnny.

'Well, he's very tame,' said Johnny's mother, 'but I don't want you to open the big door of his cage at all. Remember he isn't ours. It would be a great pity to lose him.'

Every morning Johnny gave Nippy fresh water. Every morning Johnny checked Nippy's bird-seed.

'Johnny! Johnny!' called Johnny's mother. 'Where have you got to?'

'I'm just getting Nippy some sow thistle,'

came Johnny's voice from a weedy part of the garden.

'Hey, Johnny, where are you?' shouted Mack.

'Cutting a piece of apple for Nippy,' answered Johnny from the kitchen.

Every three days Johnny cleaned out Nippy's cage. He wanted to show his mother just how well he could look after a budgie.

'Johnny, where are you?' cried Cathie down the hall.

'Talking to Nippy!' Johnny called back. 'I don't want him to be lonely while he's having his holidays.'

'I'm glad the Play Centre pet isn't an owl,' remarked Johnny's father. 'We'd have Johnny up all night catching mice for it.'

The holidays went by quickly.

'You've taken such good care of Nippy that I think we could let you have a blue budgie,' Johnny's mother said.

'We'll go and see Mr Cooney about it tomorrow.'

The first day of the new school term came round.

Johnny was trying to keep his clean first-morning-of-school clothes tidy and give Nippy fresh seed. Nippy ran backwards and forwards on his perch. His feet were wrinkled and grey, with three toes going forward and one toe going back. Once Mr Cooney had let Johnny put his hand into the Cooney budgie's cage and a blue Cooney budgie had settled on his finger. Its feet, which looked horny and cold, were light and warm. It had shuffled and bobbed and winked at Johnny.

Suddenly he wanted, very much, to feel those light warm feet again.

There was no one in the room but Cathie, and she was not watching him. Instead she was arranging her breakfast, spreading a great spoonful of honey on her toast. It took only a moment to open the big door of the cage. Johnny slid his hand in and pressed a clean first-morning-of-school finger against Nippy's green chest. Nippy stepped onto Johnny's finger. His grey feet were just as small and light as Johnny remembered.

Slowly Nippy walked over Johnny's hand, going sideways with his head tilted. Then, he did a quick little dance, and before Johnny knew what was happening, Nippy had slid up across his wrist and was out of the cage door. His wings fluttered wildly. Nippy was flying round and round the room, and there was nothing Johnny could do but stand and stare. Cathie stared too. Two pairs of round blue eyes followed the green budgie round and round and round. Nippy landed on the light cord. He hung there staring back at them. It was terrible. In another moment Johnny knew his mother would come in. She would know that Johnny had opened the big door of the Play

Centre cage and had let the Play Centre
budgie out. There would be no blue
Cooney budgie for Johnny unless Nippy
could be caught and returned to his cage
before Play Centre time.

Nippy took off again, whirring round the
room. He flew lower this time and settled
on the curtain rail.

'Climb on a chair and catch him,' breathed

Cathie. Johnny scrambled onto a chair, but before his hand was anywhere near Nippy, off Nippy flew, round and round and round. His wings made a busy breathing sound in the still room. Johnny began to run backwards and forwards beneath him. Nippy flew lower and lower and lower as if his wings were getting tired. He landed on the table.

'Johnny!' cried Cathie. Nippy had landed on her piece of toast.

The toast was thickly spread with honey.

Nippy could not get his feet out of it.

In a moment Johnny had caught him again. Holding him very gently he wiped Nippy's tiny honey feet with his clean first-day-of-school handkerchief. When most of the honey was off he slipped the little bird back into the Play Centre cage.

'Gosh!' mumbled Cathie, staring at her toast. 'I don't think this toast is good any more. I thought it was salt you had to put on the tail for catching birds.'

'Honey on the feet is better,' said Johnny, beginning to grin again, though his grin felt stiff on his face as if it was a new one he was wearing for the first time.

'Should we tell?' asked Cathie.

'If any one asks we have to tell,' Johnny answered carefully.

Cathie nodded to herself.

'No one will ask,' she murmured, and began licking her sticky fingers.

The door opened and their mother came in.

'Haven't you finished yet?' she cried.

'I have really,' said Cathie. 'The trouble was – too much toast.'

'Put it in the hen's dish in the kitchen,' said mother. 'The hens will love it.'

'They'd better not stand on it,' said Cathie very seriously.

A minute later they were ready to go. Mother and Cathie were off to Play Centre. Mack and Johnny were off to school. Mother was carrying Nippy in his Play Centre cage. Just as they were about to step off Nippy looked through the bars of his cage at Johnny.

'Johnny!' he shouted, 'Johnny! Johnny! Johnny! Where are you?'

'Oh!' gasped Johnny. 'He called me. He called my name.'

'Oh dear!' said Johnny's mother. 'Just what do we do now?'

For Johnny suddenly knew that he did not want a blue Cooney budgie at all. He wanted Nippy, that wicked green Nippy, who could call his name. His mother seemed to understand this, for she smiled and then began to laugh a little bit.

'Off to school,' she said. 'We'll talk about it after school.'

When Johnny came home that afternoon

a voice shouted at him as soon as he came into the room.

'Johnny! Johnny! Where's Johnny!'

Nippy was in his usual place as green and dancing as ever. However, he had a new cage, even larger than the Play Centre one, with a swing and two seed boxes.

His feet were covered in seed husks.

'He's wearing boots,' said Cathie. Her round blue eyes were smiling. 'Mum bought a blue Cooney budgie for the Play Centre so we are allowed to keep Nippy for always. Aren't you pleased?'

'Of course I am,' Johnny answered. 'He is the one I wanted after all.'

'He can come out of his cage and fly around the room now he's a member of the family,' Cathie went on.

'If we can work out how to catch him again,' said their mother, 'though he is so tame he will usually go back to his cage himself after a while.'

'No need to worry anyway, Mum,' said Johnny, beginning to laugh. 'Cathie could catch him in her breakfast bird trap.'

And with Nippy listening and shouting encouragement Johnny and Cathie began to tell their mother about the honey-and-budgie-breakfast adventures.

Looking for a Ghost

Running along the footpath, fire in his feet, came Sammy Scarlet. He ran on his toes, leaping as he ran, so that he seemed to dance and spin through the twilight like a grey, tumbling bird learning to fly. Sammy leaped as he ran to keep himself brave. He was going to a haunted house. That evening he was going to see a ghost for the first time in his life.

The haunted house was along a city street. It was the last house left in the street, falling to pieces in the middle of a garden of weeds. The glass in the windows was broken, and some of them were crossed

44

over with boards. There was a tall fence round it, but in some places the fence was tumbling down.

'They'll put a bulldozer through that old place soon,' said the man in the shop at the corner. 'That's a valuable piece of land. It's commercial!'

'Haunted?' Sammy had asked.

'They say there's a ghost, but it only comes out in the evening after the shops have shut up and most people have gone home. I've never seen it,' said the man in the corner shop, 'and I'm not hanging around here after half past five just to watch some ghost. Only a little one too, they say.'

'A twilight ghost,' Sammy said to himself, and felt as if something breathed cold on the back of his neck, and whispered with cold lips in his ear.

Now he ran swiftly through the early evening. Sammy had chosen his time carefully . . . not so dark that his mother

45

would worry about him, not too light for a small, cold ghost.

'Just a quick prowl around!' thought Sammy, as he ran and leaped to keep away the fear which ran beside him like a chilly, pale-eyed dog.

'If I go back now, I'm a coward,' thought Sammy, and leaped again. 'I've promised myself to see a ghost and I'm *going* to see a ghost.'

He knew the street well, but evening changed it. It took him by surprise, seeming to have grown longer and emptier. And at the end of the street the haunted house was waiting. Sammy could see its gate and its tired tumbledown fence. By the gate something moved softly. Sammy leaped in his running, matching his jump to the jump of his heart. But the shadow by the gate was only a little girl bouncing a ball with a stick. She looked up as Sammy came running towards her.

'Hello,' she said. 'I thought no one ever came here in the evening.'

'I've come,' Sammy answered, panting. 'I'm going to see the ghost.'

The little girl looked at him with shadowy black eyes. 'A real ghost?' she asked. 'What ghost?'

'A ghost that haunts this house,' Sammy replied. He was glad of someone to talk to, even a girl with a striped rubber ball in one hand and a stick in the other. She looked back at the house.

'Is this house haunted?' she asked again. 'I suppose it looks a bit haunted. It's got cobwebs on it, and thistles in the garden. Aren't you frightened of the ghost, then?'

'I'm not scared of ghosts,' said Sammy cheerfully. (He hoped it sounded cheerful.) 'They can be pretty scary to some people but, I don't know how it is, somehow they don't scare me. I'm going through the fence to take a look. They say it is only a little one.'

'Why don't you try the gate?' suggested the girl, pushing at the gate with her stick. It creaked open. Sammy stared.

'That's funny,' he said. 'I looked at the gate earlier and it was locked.'

'I'll come with you,' said the girl. 'My name is Belinda, and I would like to see a ghost too.'

'I don't think you'd better,' replied Sammy, frowning, 'because ghosts can be pretty horrible, you know . . . with sharp teeth and claws and cackling laughs. Bony too!'

'There's nothing wrong with being bony,' said Belinda.

She was very thin with a pale, serious face and long brown hair. Though she did not smile she looked friendly and interested. Her heavy shoes made her legs look even thinner, and her dress was too big for her, Sammy thought. Certainly it was too long, giving her an old-fashioned look.

'If it's scary to be bony,' said Belinda, 'I might frighten the ghost. Anyway the gate is open and I can go in if I want to.' She stepped into the old garden and Sammy stepped after her, half cross because she was coming into his private adventure, half pleased to have company. As he came through the gate Sammy felt a cold breath fall on the back of his neck. Turning round slowly he saw nothing. Perhaps it was just a little cool wind sliding into the empty garden with them.

'A garden of thistledown and dandelions,' Belinda cried. 'A garden all for birds and beetles and ghosts.' She seemed to like what she saw. 'The lawn is almost as tall as my shoulder. A ghost could easily be in that long grass, and just rise up beside us like smoke.'

Sammy glanced thoughtfully at the grass, half expecting a smoky shape to billow up and wave its arms at him. But - no smoke, no sound. It was all very still. He could hear cars out on the main road, but they seemed like thin dreams of sound, tiny flies buzzing far away. He walked up the brick path and stood on the front steps of the haunted house, looking at its sad veranda. One of the carved posts was crumbling down and the veranda sagged with it.

'You'd feel cruel just standing on this

veranda,' Sammy remarked. 'It looks so limp and sick.'

'Cruelty to verandas!' said Belinda seriously. 'Stand on it lightly, Sammy, and we'll go inside. I think a ghost would be more likely to be inside, don't you?'

'The door will be locked, won't it?' Sammy said. Then, 'How did you know my name?' he asked, looking puzzled.

'You *look* like a Sammy,' was all she said. She pushed the door and it slowly opened, like a black mouth opening to suck them into its shadows.

'I might stay out here,' Sammy said. 'The floor could cave in or something.' His voice was quiet and squashed small by the heavy silence of the whole house and garden.

'You don't have to be afraid,' Belinda told him kindly. 'It's just an old, empty house, and old houses were made of good wood.' Through the dark door she slid and vanished. Sammy *had* to follow her. Then he got the most terrible fright. He was standing in a hall so dim and dusty that he could see almost nothing. But what he *could* see was a dim and dusty figure at the other end of the hall moving slowly towards him.

'The ghost!' cried Sammy.

Belinda looked back at him. He could not see her face properly, but for some reason he thought she might be smiling.

'It isn't a ghost,' she told him. 'It's a mirror. There's a tall cupboard at the end with a mirror in its door. It's your own reflection that's frightening you.'

Sammy blinked and saw that what she said could be true. They walked cautiously up the hall. The mirror reflected the open doorway behind them. It was so dark inside that the evening outside looked bright and pearly.

Sammy rubbed his finger across the mirror.

The mirror moved and they heard a low moaning.

'The ghost!' gasped Sammy again, but it was just the cupboard door. It was a little bit open, and creaking when Sammy touched it.

'Come upstairs!' Belinda said. 'They were nice, once, these stairs. They used to be polished every day.'

'How can you tell?' asked Sammy, looking up the dark stairway.

'They are smooth under the dust,' Belinda replied, 'smooth with feet walking, and hands polishing. But that was a long time ago.'

'How can you see your way upstairs?' Sammy asked. 'It's so dark.'

'There's enough light,' she answered, already several steps above him. Sammy came after her. Out of the dark came a hand, soft and silent as the shadows, and laid silken fingers across his face.

'The ghost!' cried Sammy for the third time.

'Cobwebs, only cobwebs!' called Belinda back to him. Sammy touched his face. His own fingers, stiff with fright, found only cobwebs, just as Belinda had said. He stumbled and scrambled up after her onto the landing. There was a window boarded over. It was easy to peep through the cracks and look over the thistly garden and down the empty street.

'There used to be grass there,' Belinda whispered, peering out. 'Grass and cows. But that was a long time ago.' She straightened up. 'Come through *this* door,' she said in her ordinary voice.

Sammy did not want to be left behind. They went through the door into a small room. The boards had partly slipped away from the windows. Evening light brightened the walls and striped the ceiling. There were the remains of green curtains and a rocking-chair with one rocker broken. Sitting in the chair was a very old doll. It looked as if someone had put it down and had gone out to play for a moment. The doll seemed to expect someone to be back to play with it. Sammy looked over to the doll and around the room, and then out through the window. 'There's no ghost,' he said, 'and it's getting late. I'll have to be going.'

The ghost did not seem as important as it had a moment ago, but Sammy thought he would remember the silent, tumbling house and its wild garden, long after he had stopped thinking about ghosts.

They went down the stairs again and Sammy did not jump at the cobwebs. They went past the mirror and he creaked the cupboard door on purpose this time. Now the sound did not frighten him. It was gentle and complaining, not fierce or angry.

'It only wants to be left alone,' Belinda said, and that was what it sounded like.

They walked down the hall and Sammy turned to wave goodbye to his reflection before he shut the door. The reflection waved back at him from the end of a long tunnel of shadow. Outside, the evening darkened. Stars were showing.

'No ghost!' said Sammy, shaking his head.

They walked to the gate.

'Will you be coming back some other night to look for the ghost?' Belinda asked.

'I don't think so,' Sammy answered. 'I don't really believe in ghosts. I just thought there might be one. I've looked once and there isn't one and that's enough.'

He turned to run off home, but something made him stop and look sharply at Belinda.

'Did you see *your* reflection in that mirror?' he asked curiously. 'I don't remember your reflection.'

Belinda did not answer his question. Instead she asked him one of her own.

'Everyone has a reflection, don't they?' It was hard to see her in the late evening, but once again Sammy thought she might be smiling.

'You went up the stairs first,' he went on. 'Why didn't you brush the cobwebs away?'

'I'm not as tall as you,' Belinda said.

Sammy peered at her, waiting for her to say something more. Just for a moment, very faintly, he felt that chilly breeze touch the back of his neck again.

'No ghost!' he said at last. 'No such things as ghosts!' Then, without a goodbye, he ran off home, rockets in the heels of his shoes.

Belinda watched him go.

'The question is,' she said to herself, 'whether he would recognize a ghost, supposing he saw one.'

She went back through the gate and locked it carefully after her. She was already faint and far off in the evening, and as she pushed the bolt home she disappeared entirely.

The Witch Doctor

There was once a young man called Tom
whose father was a doctor and he wanted
Tom to be a doctor too.

Tom did not want to be a doctor. He
wanted to write poetry.

All day, all night, words sang in his
thoughts like birds in a forest. When the
wind blew Tom heard a giant shouting
enchanted words of power. When the sun
shone Tom tried to shine too, speaking out
strong golden words.

Tom should have been a poet BUT
'You must be a doctor too,' said his father.
'Those are my orders.' Tom had to turn

round and study to be a medical man. Poor Tom!

'What is this?' said the professor who was teaching the young men to be doctors. 'Someone has written me a poem. I wanted a list of different sorts of bones.'

'Well,' said Tom, 'I could not remember the names of the bones.'

'If someone came to you with a broken leg, would you read him a poem?' said the professor with great and dreadful scorn.

'Well, it might be better than nothing,' said Tom. 'And people have dreams as well as bones.'

'Young man,' said the professor, 'you will never make a doctor. It is people's bones you should think of, not their dreams.'

But Tom worked hard.

He learned all the bones.

He learned all the muscles.

He made songs of them and sang them to himself until he knew them by heart.

After several goes he passed the exam.

At last, Tom became a doctor.

The trouble was, Tom was not a very good doctor.

Nothing he did turned out well.

He got his medicines mixed up. He got spots and swellings mixed up too. He gave chickenpox people measles medicine. He gave mumps people lumps medicine.

When he should have been reading books about stomach-aches Tom was writing poetry.

After a while no one came to him unless they wanted him to write a poem for the birthday of some rich aunt.

Tom did not charge for a poem. He thought poetry should be free.

One night he sat at home just starving and writing poetry. It was a cold night, and there were cracks in the walls of his old house.

He had many of the cracks covered by poems pasted on the wall and the poems helped to keep him warm. Tom wrote busily.

'Up in a meadow close to the sea
Girls in bright dresses came dancing with
   me.'

He pulled his coat round him and imagined the meadow by the sea, the hot, hot sunshine, the tall blue flowers and the girls in their swirling skirts, like summer butterflies. The meadow seemed more real than the cold room with poems pasted all over the walls.

Tom smiled. Just as he smiled there was a loud ring at his doctor's bell on the front door.

Tom opened the door. There stood an old woman as sharp as a thorn. She wore a pointed hat and a black cloak. She carried an

enormous broomstick. Even in the light of his candle Tom could see that she was very plain and spattered with spots.

'Are you the doctor?' she asked.

'Yes,' said Tom, 'I am a doctor, but I must warn you that I'm not a very good one.'

The old woman peered at him.

'You don't look very good,' she agreed.

'How are you with spots? I want you to cure mine.'

'What's wrong with them?' asked Tom cautiously.

'Can't you see!' snapped the old woman. 'They ruin my beauty.'

'Oh no!' said Tom politely. 'True beauty always shines through any number of spots.'

The old woman simpered. 'Oh well, no doubt you're right,' she said, 'but I demand to be cured of them all the same. No girl likes to share her face with a lot of spots.'

'I can't promise anything,' Tom stammered, thinking sadly of his sunny dream, the bright girls and the leaping sea. 'I've never been very successful with spots.'

The old woman bounced in Tom's door like a wicked black frog.

'You'd better be successful with mine,' she said, 'or I'll want to know the reason why.'

She spoke in a very ominous voice, a

crackling, spitting voice, as if she was frying her words in very hot fat.

Tom jumped back as if he had been stung.

He started mixing up some medicine. 'Now was it that pink powder that was so good for spots, or was it that blue fizzy stuff?' he muttered. He mixed away with shaking hands.

He mixed a tall purple medicine for the spotty old woman. It smelled terrible.

'I wish I felt sure it would work,' Tom muttered.

But the old lady snatched it from him and swigged it down with a flick and a swish. It sounded like bath water gurgling down a plughole.

'Very tasty!' she said at last, smacking her lips.

It was at this very moment Tom remembered something. Horrible horrors! That blue fizzy stuff was meant for sprained ankles – not spots.

Tom turned cold all over. He wondered how he could explain this mistake, though it was a mistake any doctor who happened also to be a poet could make. He cleared his throat.

'Have you ever had a sprained ankle?' he asked.

But as he spoke he noticed a remarkable thing. The spots were fading.

They got smaller and smaller.

They vanished entirely.

Tom was astonished. It was the first time he had cured anybody of anything.

The old woman saw her reflection in the side of Tom's own whistling kettle. She leaped up with a joyous cry.

'Gone!' she exclaimed. 'My radiant beauty has come back better than before.'

She was highly delighted. She gave Tom a small bag of gold, and went off chuckling and telling Tom she would recommend him to her friends. Dr Tom was left on his own.

He looked hard at the bottle of blue fizzy stuff. He looked hard at the bag of gold. Then he shrugged his shoulders and went back to his poem. He let sunshine creep around him once more, and in his mind he danced with silken summer girls to the hush and sigh of the sea.

It wasn't long before there came another ring on his doctor's bell and another sharp old woman stood there in a sharp hat and sharp shoes, with sharp eyes peering back at him. She had a swollen face.

Tom cured her (with a lotion in which he mixed gunpowder by mistake).

'Very good! Very good!' she said. 'I haven't known such medical success before. We witches find it hard to get a doctor.'

'Witches!' cried Tom amazed.

'Why yes – you're a natural-born witch doctor, didn't you know? Medicine works backwards with witches so a usual doctor isn't much good to us,' said the witch.

She gave Tom a bag of gold and went out still patting her face.

'My radiant beauty has come back at last,' Tom heard her saying as she went out.

Tom stood there uneasily. 'I haven't heard the last of this,' he thought.

Somehow he knew it was no use sitting down to write more poetry. His poetry was quite gone. He went to bed instead.

In the morning when Tom woke up he knew straight away that he was worried. It took him a moment to remember what he was worried about.

Witches! He had been curing witches.

He lay in bed and worried for five exact minutes. Then he thought, 'Even a man who has been curing witches has to have breakfast.'

He got up and set his breakfast table. Then he went to see what he had in his cupboard.

Well! Three lemons and a tin of sardines!

Not much for a man who has worn himself out the night before writing poetry and curing witches of spots.

Tom was considering, when a ring sounded on the doctor's bell. Tom frowned. Could it be another witch? Could it be the police? Did you get a chance to write poetry if you were put in prison for witch curing?

He went to the door and opened it boldly. There stood the beautiful Sabina.

'Sardines for breakfast?' she asked him, smiling.

'And for lunch,' Tom answered, 'and for dinner too.'

Tom looked at her.

She had golden hair, but so pale a gold it was almost silver. She had blue eyes, but so dark a blue they were almost purple. She had a pink and white skin, and in the middle of her face a very red nose.

As Tom looked at her she sneezed twenty-seven times.

'I know you are good with spots and swellings,' she said. 'What are you like with sneezes?'

She was just so beautiful, in spite of her red nose, that Tom tried hard to think how to mix sneeze medicine. Meanwhile Sabina began to read all the poems pasted over the cracks in the walls. Her sneezing made quite a breeze and some poems blew off the walls. Soon the air was filled with whirling poetry.

Tom frowned and drummed his fingers. What was good for sneezes?

The beautiful Sabina blinked her purple eyes.

'You need a good housekeeper,' she said. 'I think I will come and housekeep for you.'

'Then I must cure you,' Tom replied, grinning a little bit. 'I know,' he said. 'I'll make you a lemon drink with my three lemons. My medicine works only with the wrong people. A lemon drink will be as good as anything for you.'

'You write interesting poetry,' said the beautiful Sabina. 'I like this one,

'Up in a - *Achoo!* - close to the sea
Girls in bright - *achoos!* - come dancing with me.'

71

'That isn't quite how I meant it to sound,' said Tom.

He must have had a good way of squeezing lemons. He made a splendid three-lemon lemon drink which cured the sneezes straight away. Then the beautiful Sabina began tidying the house and Tom sat down and began writing poetry.

'Where did you get that broom?' Tom asked, looking up for a moment.

'Oh, I always bring my own with me,' the beautiful Sabina answered.

A moment later when Tom was working out a very tricky rhyme for 'hyena' there came a loud knocking at his door.

'Come out! Come out!' voices shouted. 'We know what you've been up to. You've been curing witches!'

Tom sighed. 'Real trouble this time,' he said mournfully. Then he opened his door.

There stood the mayor, the councillors, the policeman and a crowd of people.

'*There* you are! *There* you are!' they shouted.

'You have been curing witches,' said the mayor. 'It is useless to deny it.'

'Well, perhaps I have cured one or two,' Tom admitted, 'but I did not know they were witches.'

'The witches round here,' said the mayor, 'are a very spiteful lot. And that is when they are merely poorly. Now they are well they will be a hundred times worse. There's no room in this town for a doctor who goes around curing witches. You will have to leave and we are here to make you go.'

'But I can't leave this house,' cried Tom. 'All my poetry is pasted over the holes and cracks in the walls. I can't leave my collected writings behind.'

An angry, ominous murmur rose from the people before him. 'Get rid of him! Get rid of him!' they shouted. 'Get that witch doctor out of town.'

73

The policeman sprang up the steps and seized Tom by his shirt. Tom struggled but he had had no breakfast – not even sardines. The policeman had had eggs and bacon and a sausage, followed by toast and milky coffee and a kiss from his wife. He was feeling tremendously strong. There is no doubt he would have overwhelmed Tom and carried him off to jail, but something unexpected happened.

The beautiful Sabina came out of the door behind him. She was so beautiful that all that angry crowd grew quiet. The policeman stayed holding Tom up in the air.

'Good morning,' said the beautiful Sabina. She smiled at them with her pink lips and her purple eyes. 'What are you doing with Dr Tom?'

'We're chasing him out of town,' said the mayor after a moment. 'He's been curing witches.'

'But that's wonderful!' said the beautiful Sabina. 'You won't have any more trouble from witches now. Witches are quite amiable when they are feeling well.'

Everyone stared at her.

The mayor shuffled his feet nervously. 'Do you know that for a fact?' he asked. 'I thought their wickedness would get worse.'

'Oh no!' Sabina replied in a surprised voice. 'When they are well, witches concentrate on cackling, dancing and having lively witch parties. Wickedness in witches often comes from spots or indigestion. Besides, now you have a witch doctor in town, witches will come from far and wide bringing trade with them. They will spend money in the shops, buying lively scarves, beads and other pretty trinkets.'

The mayor looked thoughtful. He himself, when he was not being mayor, had a fancy-goods shop full of scarves, beads and trinkets.

'Perhaps we are being hasty,' he said. 'This wants looking into.'

'We don't want to do anything rash,' said a councillor.

'No,' said the beautiful Sabina, 'because if I was a witch – *if* I was a witch – I would be very angry to find a mayor and town council had chased a perfectly good witch doctor out of town.'

The beautiful Sabina's voice sounded quite ominous, in a beautiful way, almost as if she just might really have been a witch herself.

'We'll have to have a meeting about this,' said the mayor. 'Constable, put that witch doctor down.'

They marched off, leaving Tom and the beautiful Sabina staring after them.

The beautiful Sabina beckoned Tom into the kitchen. There, in the middle of the table, was a big three-tier-top cake wonderfully iced and decorated with lilies and roses made out of icing.

'Just a little thing I baked up,' said the beautiful Sabina modestly.

'All from a tin of sardines?' asked Tom suspiciously.

'Oh well, I've learned how to mix things and fix things,' said the beautiful Sabina.

'It looks like a wedding cake,' Tom remarked.

'So it does,' cried Sabina in surprise. 'I was trying to remember what it looked like.'

'And,' Tom went on boldly, 'it seems a pity, having a wedding cake in the house, to waste it.'

'That's a poetical thought, Tom,' said the beautiful Sabina, smiling at him with her purple eyes.

So Tom and the beautiful Sabina were married absolutely straightaway.

The mayor and the councillors and the

policeman came to the wedding. There were some strange old women in pointed hats, too, but everyone was too polite to ask who they were. Everyone just said very politely how well they looked.

'There's a good doctor in this town,' the old women replied, giving sharp sideways glances. 'We hope he stays here. We'll get very cross if he doesn't.'

So Tom stayed in his house where the walls were covered in poems. All day he wrote poetry and each night he cured a few witches. He grew rich and was able to afford a proper doctor's car.

The beautiful Sabina helped him. She wore a nurse's cap when he was doctoring and corrected the spelling of his poetry when he was writing. Some children said they had seen her riding off on her broomstick to witch parties, but their elders only said, 'So what?'

'It's not every doctor that things work out

so well for,' Tom said, 'and not every poet either.'

The beautiful Sabina smiled with her pink lips and her purple eyes.

And they lived happily ever after.

A Tall Story

Susan was the family storyteller, and
Richard was the family listener. She told the
stories and he always listened.

But when Uncle Ted came to call, it
turned out he was a storyteller too, and
Richard stopped listening to Susan. He
listened to Uncle Ted all the time, one story
after another.

'Tell a story, Uncle Ted!' demanded
Richard.

'Don't start him off again,' begged
Susan. 'I think it's bad to encourage
him.'

'Just one little story,' Richard begged.

Uncle Ted leaned back and looked up at the ceiling, as storytellers do.

'I think I've told most of my stories,' he said. 'Let me see! I've told you about the mystery treasure of Bones Island, haven't I?'

'That was a good one,' Richard answered, smiling and remembering.

'Oh yes . . . and I've told you about the time I was nearly married to the Queen of the Bird People?'

'She lived in a big royal nest, didn't she?' Richard nodded. 'And laid eggs.'

'What about the catching of the Great Christmas Tree Thieves – a smart bit of detective work on my part?' Uncle Ted asked, thinking hard. 'All the thieves were dressed as Santa Claus.'

'Hasn't anything happened to you since then?' Richard asked.

'Nothing, nothing,' said Uncle Ted sadly. 'Except, of course, for the hunting of the giant land-dwelling oyster. You'll remember the headlines in the paper, no doubt. You may even have seen it on TV.'

'You don't hunt oysters,' Susan said snappily. 'You fish for them. You know you fish for them, Uncle Ted.'

'Those are the small ones,' Uncle Ted replied carelessly. 'This was a large one ... enormous! ... a horrible amorphous creature as big as a town hall ... a land-dwelling oyster.'

'It couldn't be,' Susan said sternly. 'No oyster could be as big as a town hall.'

'Tell me!' begged Richard. 'Tell a story.'

So Uncle Ted began: 'This dreadful monster had taken to coming out at night, and snatching up all kinds of midnight travellers. Five vans of buns and assorted sweets on their way to a southern carnival had vanished off the face of the earth. Two brass bands, a travelling circus, a mobile library and an army lorry filled with angry sergeant-majors had entirely disappeared ...

We couldn't let it continue. A creature with a digestion like that had to be got rid of. No one was safe – not even town councillors. Of course, they sent for me, offering to pay richly if I disposed of the monster.'

Uncle Ted paused.

'You always make adventures pay,' said Richard. 'Go on.'

'None of it is true,' Susan muttered.

'I chose three guns . . . my trusty revolver, my rifle and my cannon. I drove towards the giant oyster's lair in my little zinger of a truck. Many oyster soup officials were standing by, with a Pre-Fabricated Re-Locatable Oyster-Soup factory. As soon as I had shot the giant oyster they would move in with a hundred oyster-soup cooks, great vats of salt and pepper, and bags of lemons. They hoped to make a year's supply of oyster soup from this dreadful monster.'

'I'll bet you planned all that,' said Richard. 'Were you getting money for it?'

'I was to get ten pence for every tin of oyster soup. They expected to sell at least twenty tins of soup a day over a year. It was a small fortune,' said Uncle Ted.

'Uncle Ted, nobody believes you,' said Susan, shaking her head.

Uncle Ted went on: 'I moved in first with a loud-speaker. From a distance of a mere two hundred yards I began making sarcastic remarks about oysters. This was to infuriate the oyster and bring it out into the daylight. Out it came . . . a great amorphous mass as big as a town hall.'

'You've already said that,' objected Susan.

'Was it horrible?' asked Richard.

'Unspeakably horrible!' Uncle Ted cried, shuddering. 'It reared up menacingly over the trees, all slimy and jelly-like with great teeth gnashing in a wide slit of a mouth.'

'Oysters don't have teeth,' Susan stated.

'They don't usually,' agreed Uncle Ted. 'I can't explain it. I'm not an oyster expert. All

I know is, this oyster came undulating towards me at surprising speed, gnashing a mouthful of very sharp-looking teeth. Perhaps it had made itself some false teeth out of oyster shell.'

'I don't know how you can bear to listen to such things,' Susan muttered to Richard, shaking her head again.

'I fired first with my trusty rifle, and then with my trusty revolver. I could not miss such a huge target, but mere bullets made no difference. Even when I fired the cannon ball right through it, it did not hesitate. I had to climb into my truck and drive off as quickly as I could.'

'But the oyster could catch trucks!' cried Susan triumphantly. 'You said it had caught an army lorry.'

'Too true!' agreed Uncle Ted. 'It nearly caught up with me, but my truck, though small, was fitted with an experimental jet engine of a revolutionary kind. Just as the

oyster (a vast amorphous mass, did I mention?) was about to swoop on me, I pressed button A and rotating helicopter blades unfolded out of the roof of my truck, whisking me out of danger. Furious at losing its prey, the terrible mollusc set up a wailing so horrible that – I give you my word – the helicopter blades nearly stopped, and I hung quivering in the air. There were a few tense moments, believe me, before I got back out of reach and the oyster gave up and slunk back to its cave.

'There was great despondency when I returned at last.

'"We'll have to declare a national emergency and call out the army," declared the town councillors. The oyster-soup officials weren't too happy about this. The army could deal with it, of course, but this meant blowing the monster to bits – thus spoiling it for soup purposes. The oyster-soup officials didn't fancy picking bits of oyster out of the trees for miles around.

'We all thought hard. A quick, cool brain is worth a million in an emergency.

'"I've got a plan," I said. "It'll cost a bit to get it under way, and if it works I'll want fifteen pence on every can of oyster-soup."

'"You drive a hard bargain," said the leading oyster-soup official. "But we have no choice. If we get this great oyster, I think we'll manage to get command of the entire oyster-soup market."

'Now,' cried Uncle Ted, 'what do you think my plan was?'

'I couldn't ever guess,' said Susan sourly. 'It could be anything.'

'Go on, Uncle Ted,' whispered Richard, staring at Uncle Ted anxiously.

'All afternoon we spent loading a council rubbish truck. The hotel gave us five kegs of beer – rather a poor brew, I'm afraid. Miss Dobbs, the vicar's sister, hearing the announcement of our plan over the radio, contributed a whole dozen bottles of her famous parsnip-and-elderberry wine. Several farmers gave large quantities of apple cider. Colonel Scobie donated several flagons of a drink of his own invention – carrot whisky, he called it. He said it helped him see in the dark, being extra rich in Vitamin A ... A Japanese family gave us a cask of saki – I think that's made from rice.

My gift was simple, but incredibly rich – simply five cases of simple French champagne that I happened to have with me.'

'Uncle Ted, your stories are all lies and boasting,' cried Susan. 'Lies! Lies!'

'Susan,' said her mother, 'you are not to call your uncle a liar. Go outside if you can't behave better.'

Susan went outside. 'Uncle or not, it's still all lies,' she told the cat. Then she hid in the garden under the open window to listen to the rest of the story.

Inside the house Uncle Ted was going on: 'Who was to drive this truck? Every eye looked hopefully at me. It was putting my head into the jaws of death yet again, but I agreed with a tired smile. We travelling adventurers are prepared for anything. Besides, I had a small fortune at stake.

'Late that night I drove the truck down the road that passed by the oyster's lair. As we had expected, the oyster charged out at the lorry. I saw its dark shape against the stars – a vast amorphous mass (as I just may have mentioned before) and I had time to slide out and hide in a ditch while the oyster, not realizing I had gone, swept by me and devoured the truck ... beer, carrot whisky, cider, parsnip wine, saki, champagne and all.

'We waited anxiously. After about a quarter of an hour the oyster began to behave in a very strange fashion. It began to sway to and fro and actually tried to sing. I can tell you, it was one of the worst half-hours of my career. I've sat through operas and many folksong recitals, but nothing, nothing to compare with the giant oyster, full of champagne and carrot whisky, trying to sing. It was drunk, of course.'

'An oyster drunk!' cried Richard, almost not believing.

'Hopelessly inebriated!' Uncle Ted said

solemnly. 'At the end of half an hour it collapsed in a quivering heap. The Pre-Fabricated Re-Locatable Oyster-Soup factory came in, the cooks got to work and – well – you're having some of it for dinner tonight, so your mother tells me.'

'Was it fair to cut it up while it was helpless?' asked Richard doubtfully.

'Not quite fair – but you can't consider fair play too strongly when you're dealing with a creature that will tackle a lorry full of sergeant-majors, you know. Besides, it must have died happy – don't forget it had just consumed a year's supply of French champagne. People tasting the soup, incidentally, comment on the delicate champagne flavour that complements the oyster so beautifully. Go out into the kitchen, and get your mother to show you the genuine tin.'

Richard ran off, and Uncle Ted could hear him shouting excitedly in the kitchen.

'Uncle Ted,' said a voice, and there was Susan. 'Uncle Ted, shall I tell you how the story really ended?'

Uncle Ted looked at her cautiously. 'I'd like to hear,' he said.

Susan began: 'There you were, driving down the road at midnight. You saw the oyster descending on the truck . . . a vast amorphous mass—'

'I like the words you choose,' interrupted Uncle Ted.

'Now, *now* was the time for you to leap out of the truck. You went to open the door. Horrors! It was locked. It was a special automatically locking door, easy to open if you knew the way, but you had forgotten to check up. The giant oyster was coming nearer and nearer and then – and then . . .'

'Yes! Yes!' whispered Uncle Ted.

'Alas, the monster leaped onto the truck and ate you all up. You struggled wildly but it was no use. Later you were turned into soup and Mother is cooking you in the kitchen right now.'

'But I seem to be still here,' objected Uncle Ted. 'I'm sure I'm here . . .'

'All ghosts feel that,' Susan said firmly. 'I'm afraid, Uncle Ted, you are a mere ghostly apparition.'

Uncle Ted and Susan looked at each other . . . They began to smile. They began to laugh.

'A much better end,' said Uncle Ted. 'I didn't realize there was another tall-storyteller in the family.'

'It's not really a better end, just a bit taller,' said Susan. 'Yours can be the right one. You laugh too hard for a ghost! Now you tell your end to the story specially for me.'

'I think it's time you told me a story,' said Uncle Ted. 'For instance, I've heard all sort of rumours about the time you were carried off by the rare Subterranean Gorilla, who had seen you swimming at the beach and had been struck by your remarkable beauty. Wouldn't you like to tell me the facts of the case? You might have time before the soup is served?'

So Susan told him the story and, as it turned out, Uncle Ted was a wonderful listener - all good storytellers have to be - even better than Richard.

Hide and Seek
in a Dark House

In and out the window
In and out the door!
Up the path and round again,
Sliding on the floor.

Breathing through the keyhole,
Whispering on the stair,
Hiding by the dust bin,
Crouching by a chair!

Now without a candle,
Turning off the light,

We're a rustling circus
Entertaining Night.

We're the circus people,
Acrobat and clown,
Pulling shadows round us
Drawing darkness down.

Only Night can see us
Flitting room to room
Wiped away by blackness
Painted out by gloom.

In and out the darkness
Who can really see?
Are the others changing?
Am I really me?

The Curiosity
Concert

Down the street, watching and wondering,
came Katie Stephenson, bringing her
curiosity with her. She looked over hedges
and through gateways. She looked up into
trees and down into gutters.

Katie Stephenson was curious about
everything – curious about streets, gardens
and houses. Curious, mostly, about people
and the different ways they lived and the
different things they had around them. To
Katie a simple walk to the shop was rather
like a small circus. Every person she passed

was doing some little act to entertain her. For instance, on the other side of the street Mrs Pope and Mrs Poole were walking together, wearing similar coats. But why was Mrs Pope wearing a big hat, and why was Mrs Poole carrying an umbrella on a perfectly fine day?

Mr J. G. Bingham – Katie knew his name, for it was on his yellow letter-box – was clipping his hedge and whistling softly to himself. Next door Mrs Floyd was smacking one of her twins. Katie watched to see if the other twin got smacked too, but Mrs Floyd marched back inside driving the bad twin before her.

Next door again was the Goodwin house. Katie came to a full stop and peered closely down the slope of the lawn, hoping the door might open and she could look into Mrs Goodwin's hall and see Mrs Goodwin's new golden carpet. But the door stayed closed. The Goodwin house was so beautiful with its long green lawn and big trees and bright garden. Vines covered its veranda and there was a tennis court poking out from the back of the house. What could it be like inside? Katie wondered. Was everything soft and fluffy and golden like the carpet? Most houses she could guess at, but the wonderful Goodwin house was not a house that a girl with tangled hair and scratched knees could guess about very well.

When she came to the shop there was Mrs Goodwin herself buying a dozen eggs and some streaky bacon. She was wearing a beautiful white trouser suit that made her shining hair look as golden as the new carpet. Katie stood as close to her as she could and sniffed at Mrs Goodwin's flowery smell. Mrs Goodwin did not notice Katie standing there, breathing deeply, staring at her as if she was learning her by heart.

'How's the boy?' asked Mr Gilbert, the shopkeeper.

'Oh, he's getting better all the time,' Mrs Goodwin replied. 'The doctor wants him in bed for three more days but – good heavens – he's sick of his room, his books, his games . . . nothing's right. I'm at my wits' end about keeping him amused, and he's so grumpy too.'

'Shows he's on the mend,' said Mr Gilbert cheerfully. 'And three days isn't so long.'

'Another three days and I'll be in bed beside him,' Mrs Goodwin sighed and walked out of the shop, flowery scent, shining hair and all, back to her beautiful house.

'Well, Katie – what can I do for you?' asked Mr Gilbert, but Katie was staring after Mrs Goodwin.

'Is it Jackie Goodwin you were talking about?'

'He's had rheumatic fever,' Mr Gilbert nodded. 'He'll have to take it quietly for a bit, I should think. It's tough on his Mum, though, because he's the sort of boy who thinks he owns the world at the best of times. I'll bet she's got her work cut out at present all right. What Jackie needs is a few brothers and sisters – no shortage of them down your way, eh Katie?'

Katie looked at Mr Gilbert for the first time. 'Mr Gilbert,' she said, 'you've given me an idea.'

In spite of her new golden carpet and her shining golden hair Mrs Goodwin was having a miserable day. Jackie wouldn't touch his scrambled eggs at lunch time.

Then he rubbed crayon into his blanket, almost, Mrs Goodwin thought, on purpose. And when she sat down to read to him a little later in the afternoon he wriggled and sighed until she stopped in the middle of

the story and shut the book with a snap.
Then Jackie cried.

'Oh, Jack!' said Mrs Goodwin, almost ready
to cry herself.

At that very moment the front door bell
rang. Mrs Goodwin went at once, but before
she reached the door the bell rang again just
as if somebody was trying it out, enjoying
its soft chime. Mrs Goodwin opened the
door. At first she thought the veranda was
full of people. Then she saw that there were
only five. Katie Stephenson was standing
there and with her were her brothers
Roddy and Tom and her two sisters, the
bigger one Barbara holding the baby one,
Catherine.

They were all dressed like people from
fairy stories. Katie wore a greeny-blue dress
with a long train dragging behind her. On
her head was a mask made to look like the
head of a bird, with a yellow beak sticking
out over her nose. Roddy was dressed as

some sort of space man. He appeared to be
covered almost entirely in cooking foil, and
his face was painted green. Barbara, in a
brown woolly jersey and tights, tail pinned
on behind and a mask with a pointed nose,
was probably meant to be a fox, but her
brown eyes were soft and anxious, quite
unfox-like, as they looked up at Mrs
Goodwin. Thomas Stephenson was six –

Jackie's own age – and he was dressed as a scarecrow with raggy clothes, a dreadful old hat and straw stuffed around his shoes, into his sleeves and down his neck, while the baby Catherine, in a long black dress and a hat like a black ice-cream cone, was the smallest witch Mrs Goodwin had ever seen.

'Blow me down!' said Mrs Goodwin weakly.

'Good afternoon, Mrs Goodwin,' Katie Stephenson began. 'I was hearing in the shop today that Jackie wanted some entertainment. We are a concert party, Mrs Goodwin, come to put on a concert specially for Jackie. It's a good deed to visit the sick and my brother Roddy is a boy scout as well as a poet, so it can count as a good deed for him, as well as amusing Jackie.' She pointed to a black case behind her. 'I've brought my mother's piano accordion which I can play on if you don't mind me being not absolutely perfect at it yet.'

Mrs Goodwin longed to tell them to go home but, even while she was thinking of kind words to say goodbye with, she thought of Jackie crying and cross in his room.

'Come on through,' she said, smiling suddenly. 'Jackie and I will really enjoy a concert. We're tired of everything else.'

The Stephensons stepped through onto her new golden carpet. Katie stared down and saw her school sandals pressing into the soft wool. She sniffed the smell of the Goodwins' house and lifted her eyes to snatch quick glimpses of pictures, a fish tank, and a grandfather clock with the sun and the moon on its face as well as all the usual numbers. At the same time Mrs Goodwin was snatching glances at the Stephensons.

'You've been to a lot of work,' she said. 'I like your costumes.'

'They're the fancy dresses we wore at the Christmas fancy dress party,' Barbara explained proudly. 'We don't get much chance to wear them.'

'I'm a peacock,' Katie said. 'Watch out for my tail, you kids.' She stared, enchanted, at the great vase of mixed flowers Mrs Goodwin had put upon her hall table only that morning.

'Jackie - you've got visitors,' Mrs Goodwin said, opening the door to Jackie's room. Jackie looked at them drearily from under cross red eyelids. But then his eyes opened wider, his mouth lifted at the corners and he sat up on his crumpled pillows. Before he could say a word Katie began. She leaped into the space at the foot of his bed and cried:

'The Stephensons are here to present their famous variety concert - hours of laughter

106

and song - something for everyone. Take your seat, madam,' she added to Mrs Goodwin; 'the curtain is up and the show is about to roll.' She bent over her black box. 'Give us a hand, Rod,' she muttered, hoisting out an old but well-polished piano accordion and struggling into the harness. At last she stood straight, her fingers on the yellowing keys. 'We will begin with a great old song, "When father painted the parlour", sung by the famous Stephenson Harmonic Songsters.'

The Stephenson Harmonic Songsters began a little shyly, but grew louder and more cheerful as the song progressed. Barbara had to put the baby Catherine down. She clung to Barbara's leg and danced by bending her knees and jigging up and down, without taking her feet off the floor. She sang too, but some song of her own that had nothing to do with father painting the parlour.

Mrs Goodwin clapped loudly and enthusiastically when the song was finished and Jackie joined in clapping and called, 'More, more!'

'And now the Stephensons will give the countdown and Roddy Stephenson will then give the actual, entire sound of a rocket taking off for Mars,' Katie announced. 'Come on, kids – ten, nine, eight, seven . . .'

The Stephensons all joined in, '. . . six, five, four, three, two, one, BLAST OFF!' they shouted. Roddy made the most remarkable sound ever heard in the Goodwin house – a kind of long shushing that slowly turned into a booming roar. His face went red, his eyes screwed up and his shoulders hunched. It seemed hard to believe that anyone's throat could produce such a noise. When he finally ran out of breath, the noise stopped, his eyes opened, he saw Mrs Goodwin looking at him in astonishment, and he started to turn red again with embarrassment. Jackie was thrilled.

'Now Roddy will recite his famous space poem. Speak up, Roddy!'

Roddy, pleased with the applause his imitation of a rocket had won, began to recite rather shyly:

'Out of my ship between the stars
I stare out into space
A thousand suns and galaxies
Look back into my face.

The suns are bright as trumpet calls,
The moons, like wind bells, chime.
I am the centre of a wheel
That spins in space and time.'

'There you are – pretty good, eh?' cried Katie. 'A poem which is going to be in the school magazine at the end of the year.

Now Barbara will do a dance . . . a dance called "The Happy Fox".'

Katie's scratched fingers began to wander gently over the keys of the piano accordion, playing 'So early in the morning'. Barbara began to twirl and sweep the air with her arms. She ran to the right. She ran to the left. Her bushy tail bounced behind her. She pretended to catch some prey, tossing it into the air and catching it again. Katie watched her proudly and played a few wrong notes. At last Barbara's dance was over. Then Katie picked up Catherine and held her cleverly with her right arm while, with her left hand, she pushed Thomas the scarecrow forward.

'Now the poem of "The Witch and the Scarecrow",' she announced. 'I'm saying this one, because it is my favourite:

'Out in the fields of tossing grass
A scarecrow saw a witch go past.

Her hair was pale as thistledown
Her tall hat had a pointed crown.

Her face was full of magic wild
She was a witch's magic child
And, softly, as she went along
She sang a strange enchanted song.

The scarecrow could not say a word
Of what he'd seen and what he'd heard,
He stood all day the corn amid
And kept the witch's secret hid.'

Katie did not look at Mrs Goodwin or
Jackie while she said her poem. She looked
over their heads and seemed to see,
somewhere behind them on Jackie's white
wall, the shadows of the scarecrow and the
witch in their grassy fields. Really she was
looking at Jackie's animal posters, and the
clown puppet that hung from a hook in the
corner.

'That poem,' she went on, 'was written by Roddy Stephenson, and was in last year's school magazine. And now,' she said, as Mrs Goodwin and Jackie clapped cheerfully, 'there will be a few minutes while the Stephensons get their breaths again. After that the show will continue. Sweets will be served all round at half-time.'

'I'll just go out into the kitchen for a moment,' Mrs Goodwin said. 'Call me when the concert is about to go on again.'

What with showing Jackie how to play the piano accordion, and what with Jackie showing Tom how to work the clown puppet, the half-time was rather long. Before the concert had started again Mrs Goodwin came back into the room with tea. She had made delicious white toast and covered it with scrambled egg, grated cheese and thin strips of bacon all grilled to a sizzling brown. There were slices of date square and fruitcake and glasses with orange juice and ice and a coloured straw in each glass. It was a regular party being held in Jackie's room.

'Oh boy,' cried Roddy. 'I haven't seen such a tea since Mum got her job.'

'Or even before,' said Katie. 'Mum doesn't do much cooking, not the cake sort of cooking. She's good on spaghetti, but not so good on cakes.'

'She doesn't like sewing much either,' said Barbara.

Jackie looked interested. 'What does she like doing?' he asked.

'She likes poetry and dancing,' said Tom. 'She can sing and play the guitar and the piano accordion.'

'She likes to go on picnics,' said Barbara.

'Last time Mum made a cake we took it on a picnic and had it for pudding. We called it Picnic Pudding Cake,' Roddy added, taking another slice of date square.

'I wish I had some of that cake,' Jackie remarked wistfully. Then he ate toast covered with cheese, bacon and the scrambled eggs he had refused for lunch.

After the refreshments the concert continued. The first item was Tom, standing on his head, dropping straw everywhere, and singing 'What shall we do with a drunken sailor?' The second item was riddles, which Mrs Goodwin and Jackie had to answer because the Stephensons knew the answers already. The third item was a dance. Katie played 'Hands, Knees and Boomps-a-daisy' on the piano accordion. Roddy danced with Barbara and Tom tried to dance with Catherine. But after a little while Mrs Goodwin got up and danced with Tom because Catherine preferred to do a little jumping dance of her own. Jackie longed to join in.

'Next week, Jackie. Next week!' called
Katie cheerfully.

To finish the concert she played 'Waltzing
Matilda', which was the tune she knew best,
and everyone, even Jackie, was able to join
in on this last item.

'And now,' cried Katie, her voice sounding
rather hoarse, 'the Stephenson concert party
is over. The Stephensons have to go home

and put the vegetables on. But don't worry, friends – they'll be back.'

'Will you really?' Jackie demanded. 'Will you be back tomorrow?'

'Do come!' Mrs Goodwin said, and you could see that she meant it. 'It's been wonderful for Jackie, and I've enjoyed the concert too.'

Katie looked uncertain. Then she smiled. 'Oh, we'll probably be able to drop in,' she replied in a lordly fashion. 'The show must go on.'

The Stephensons left Jackie and his mother much more cheerful than they had found them.

As they went along Barbara said, 'That was a good idea of yours, Katie. It's fun doing good deeds.'

'Don't take too much notice of her good-deed talk,' replied Roddy, looking sternly at Katie. 'It was just an excuse to get into the Goodwin house. She's been mad with curiosity about that house for months and months.'

'So what!' Katie said, turning up her nose. 'I *like* being curious.'

The Boy
who Bounced

Once there was a little boy who had a very
bad habit indeed. He used to bounce like a
ball. Wherever he went his mother would
say:

'Walk like a little gentleman.' But he
wouldn't. He bounced instead. His father
said:

'No one in our family has ever bounced
before. I wish you would do something else.
You could run a bit, or even hop, or you
could skip.'

The little boy took no notice at all. This

was a mistake because one day he bounced on a magician who was snoozing in the sun. The magician was very cross.

'It really is too much,' he cried. 'I came out for a quiet day in the country and what happens? First I'm chased by a bull (I had to turn it into a canary bird to get away). Then I'm chased by the farmer who owned the bull (I had to change a foxglove into a lot of money to pay him). It has left me very tired. I lie down to have a snooze and a nasty little boy comes and bounces on me. Pah! Say you're sorry, little boy, and walk off quietly.'

The rude little boy took no notice of the magician. He started to bounce away. The magician became very angry indeed.

'If you want to bounce, well, bounce you shall,' he declared, and began to mutter magic words very quickly. The little boy felt suddenly strange about the fingers and toes – a sort of pins and needles feeling.

(That was the magic working.) Before he could say 'Mousetrap!' he had turned into a red rubber ball – a big ball, a bouncing ball. He could bounce so softly that he wouldn't break a cobweb if he bounced on it. He could bounce as high as a pine tree.

'Meet me here in a year's time,' the magician said, 'and I'll think about whether or not to turn you into a boy again.' Then he lay down and began to snooze once more.

The Bouncer leaped over the creek and began to go round the world. He felt quite happy because now he could bounce so much better than before. As he went past the school all the children came running out trying to catch him, but he went too fast for them. Soon he reached the sea.

He couldn't bounce very easily on the water. Instead the waves helped him along. They were delighted to have such a fine red ball to play with and they tossed him to one another until he reached Africa.

Lions opened their yellow eyes as the Bouncer went past and the giraffes stretched their necks to see him. They stretched them so far that all the giraffes in that part of Africa have longer necks than any other giraffes which makes them very proud and conceited.

He went through all sorts of countries with names I can't spell, and his fine red paint wore off so he became a grey battered-looking bouncer. He went more slowly now and had to stop to catch his breath. When he stopped, he hid. It was one day while he was hiding that he overheard two men talking.

'I hear they have caught a wicked magician,' the first man said.

'Well, I don't know if he is wicked or not,' the second man said in reply, 'but they are going to beat him. Would you like to come and watch?'

'Yes I would,' said the first man.

'How unfair!' the Bouncer thought. 'Poor magician! I shall rescue him!' He followed the men, bouncing so softly they did not hear him.

The magician was brought out from prison, and twelve men in black stood with sticks to beat him. He looked small and old

and his gingery whiskers drooped sadly.
'That isn't my magician,' the Bouncer
thought, 'but he is very like him.'

Then, just as the twelve men were lifting
their sticks to beat the magician, the
Bouncer gave a tremendous *bounce* and
knocked them all head over heels. Quick as
a cat the magician leaped onto the

Bouncer's back and off they went on great high bounces as high as the trees.

'Turn to the left,' the magician whispered. 'Then go over the river and turn to the right. We will be in another country after that and we will find my brother snoozing beside a creek.'

So the Bouncer did as he was told and, sure enough, it wasn't long before he recognized his home and the creek where he had bounced on the first magician. There the first magician was – still snoozing, with grass growing over him, looking like an old mossy log. He sat up, rubbing his eyes, as the Bouncer came along.

'What! You back so soon?' he said.

'You said to come back in a year,' the Bouncer replied, 'and I would like a change from bouncing.'

'He has been very good!' said the second magician. 'He saved me when they were going to beat me.'

'Oh well,' said the first magician, 'I suppose you can be a boy again, but you've got to walk from now on, not bounce.'

He muttered his magic words backwards and there was the boy again, only his clothes were too small for him now because he was a year taller.

He thanked the magicians, and they went one way and he the other – all the way back home. His mother frowned at him when he came in.

'You're late!' she said. 'Your dinner got cold and we had to give it to the cat.'

'I've been bouncing round the world,' said the boy. 'It's made me pretty hungry.'

'I'll make you a sandwich,' she said. 'But don't be so late again.'

So that is the story of the boy who was turned into a Bouncer. He was always very careful when he walked about after that, in case he bounced on a magician.

The Trees

Ever since Elizabeth could remember, pine trees had grown along the north fence like a line of giant green soldiers marching down the hill, but today, a bright shining blue and gold day, men were coming to cut them down.

Judith and Colin, who were both younger than Elizabeth, teased her at breakfast time. They were looking forward to the tree men coming with their axes and saws and they could not understand why Elizabeth was not excited too. The funny thing was Elizabeth could not explain it to them.

'The trees will just *crash* down!' Colin

cried. 'Like ninepins knocked over. Don't you even want to hear them crash?'

'I'll hate it!' Elizabeth cried. She felt as if every hair on her head was standing on end with anger.

'Why don't you want to hear it?' asked Judith, looking at Elizabeth with a round solemn face like a freckled owl.

'I just don't!' Elizabeth muttered. She wanted to tell Judith that she loved the tall green pine trees. When she woke up in the morning and looked out of her window they were the first things she saw. Flying above them the magpies would toss and turn in the air making their strange silvery yodelling sound like a musical box gone wrong. When the moon crept over the sky at night Elizabeth saw it through the branches of the pines, and that dark line of trees on the greeny brown hillside was her first sight of home when she came back from town. Because she had climbed them

so often she felt she knew every branch
and hollow of them by heart. They were all
her friends, but the largest tree of all was
her favourite because her swing hung from
its lowest branch. Elizabeth was growing so
tall that she had to tuck her feet under her
when she was on the swing but she still
loved swinging. Sometimes she felt the
swing might come off and fly away with

her to some magic land. It seemed terrible to think that after today she would never again swing high up and see blue sky through a crisscross of branches and twigs and pine needles. Elizabeth wanted to explain this but somehow she didn't know the right words, and even if she did she felt Colin and Judith would not understand them.

'Anyhow,' Colin said, guessing her thoughts, 'Daddy says he'll make a new swing for us like one in the park.'

'That won't be the same,' Elizabeth said scornfully. 'It will just be a dead *swing*. The one on the pine tree is alive.'

'You're as mad as mad!' Colin cried. 'Whoever heard of a live swing?'

Daddy looked at them crossly.

'Now you children!' he exclaimed. 'Stop that bickering and sniping. Elizabeth, *I'm* sorry the trees have to be cut down, too – they're seventy years old and were here when grandfather was born. But they've grown too tall – they're just not safe so close to the house any more. They've got to go. I'm not happy about it but there you are!'

'Yes, Daddy,' Elizabeth said, 'I know that,' and she tried to take no more notice of Colin and Judith, even when they whispered to each other watching her closely.

'Crash go the pine trees!'

Inside Elizabeth said to herself, 'It won't be like home ever again without the pine trees.'

After breakfast the tree fellers arrived in a truck. The back of the truck was loaded with axes and ropes and tins of lunch. And in the middle of all these things was a winch with wire rope wound round it. There were three tree fellers and they climbed out of the truck and shook hands with Elizabeth's father.

'Hello!' said the tallest man of the three,

looking at Judith and Colin. 'Have we got an audience?'

'They've been looking forward to it,' said Daddy. 'Whereas Elizabeth here wants us to keep the trees.' The tall man smiled at Elizabeth. He had white teeth and a brown crinkled face and he was wearing a blue shirt. Elizabeth liked him for a moment, then she thought to herself that he was a tree killer and she did not smile back.

'Will you chop the trees down with an axe?' asked Judith.

'No!' said the blue-shirt man. 'We'll use a chainsaw.'

'Is that a saw to saw chains through?' Judith asked again, but of course she was only five and didn't know much.

'Don't be mad!' said Colin. 'It's a big saw with a motor on it, isn't it? You don't have to push and pull it – the motor drives it and makes it cut, doesn't it?'

'That's right,' said the blue-shirt man. 'I can

see you know all about it. Now, let's have a look at these sticks!'

'Sticks!' Colin yelled. 'It's trees you've got to cut down – not sticks!'

'We call the trees sticks,' the blue-shirt man said. 'It stops us from being too frightened of them. It's dangerous cutting down trees, you know. They try to fall on us but we're too clever for them. We make them fall where we want them to.'

Elizabeth followed them as they all set off together to look at the trees.

'Sticks!' she thought. 'What a name for lovely green trees!' She watched with a mixed feeling of being interested and sad while the man fastened ropes to the first tree in the line. Then the blue-shirted man started up his chainsaw. It roared like a lion until he cut into the tree with it. Then it screamed furiously and the sawdust flew out around the head and shoulders of the blue-shirt man. First he cut a piece out of one side of the tree and then he moved around to the other side where the chain-saw screamed and the sawdust flew again Then he stood back and shouted.

'All right – give her a go.'

The truck engine started up and moved forward by inches. The rope grew tight. Staring at the tree top Elizabeth saw it move as if there was a wind in it – a wind that the

other pine trees could not feel. Then it started to fall. Elizabeth held her breath. It fell slowly at first, then faster and faster until it smashed onto the ground with a sound like crashing drums, thunder and tearing sheets. Branches broke. Pine cones flew into the air like startled birds. Judith and Colin screamed with delight.

'Didn't it crash! Gee! Didn't it crash!' yelled Colin.

'I thought it was scratching the sky down!' Judith cried. Elizabeth did not know what to say. It had been exciting to see the tree falling - to see all that great tower of needles, cones, and branches coming down at her (though of course it hadn't landed anywhere near her). Yet now there was a gap in the line of trees like a tooth missing in a smile. She felt sad again.

The chainsaw screamed and the truck engine rumbled. Neighbours came to stare. Tree after tree came tumbling down.

They lay in a great tangled mass of broken branches and oozing pine gum, smelling of the gum and bruised pine needles. They weren't part of a grand row of trees any more – they were just a mess.

Then it was lunch time. The men got their lunch tin and sat down to eat. Colin and Judith sat down beside them talking, while Elizabeth lurked a little way off, not wanting to join in, but not wanting to miss out on anything. Suddenly the blue-shirt man looked over Colin's head, straight at her.

'You're quiet today, lassie,' he said. 'So you're sorry to lose the trees!' Before Elizabeth could reply he went on: 'Think it's sad m'self to see those sticks come down, but some of them are old and tired, really dangerous. And don't you go thinking you're losing out altogether. You're losing the trees, sure, but look at the view. We're not just cutting down trees for your Dad – we're letting in the world.'

Elizabeth looked at the view. Up till now she had just been seeing it as a space where pine trees had been growing. Now she realized she could see right across the valley from her own hillside to the great greeny-brown hills opposite. In between lay farms and fields and the winding line of the creek with its fringe of poplars and willows. She could see the dark green shapes of the pine trees and firs, and the small white shapes of the sheep with their shadows beside them, short and stumpy because it was midday. Elizabeth had a feeling of space and sky she had never had before. Deep down inside her she knew that she would come to love this even more than she had loved her pine trees.

She looked at the blue-shirt man and smiled uncertainly.

During the afternoon when more of the trees came down Elizabeth looked at the widening space they left with a different feeling. She saw still more of the hills and the widening wandering creek come out from behind the pine trees. The new view was like a butterfly struggling out of its chrysalis – something gained not lost.

At last there was only the swing tree left. Elizabeth did not want to watch it fall. She went inside but all the time her ears were listening for the crash. It did not come. Instead she heard the truck starting up and going away again. When she looked out of the window she saw her new wide view and at the very end of it a single green soldier stood on guard – the swing tree.

Out ran Elizabeth into the kitchen where Colin and Judith were eating bread and jam. When Colin saw her he said:

'Anyhow, they didn't cut down your old swing tree, so there. It's still a strong tree and not anywhere near the house, so the blue-shirt man asked Daddy and Daddy said to leave it.'

'It was the biggest tree of all,' said Judith, but Elizabeth scarcely heard her. She ran out into the yard. It was not easy to get to the swing tree now, for the back of the yard was filled with the fallen pines, but Elizabeth wove her way over and under the grey trunks and branches. At last she stood under the old tree. She touched the swing dangling from it. She looked up at the sky

through its branches and felt its rough bark under her hand.

'Hello!' she said softly. 'Are you still here?' Then she got on the swing and worked her way up high sweeping backwards and forwards in an long swooping line. Above her the pine tree rustled and whispered as if it was talking to her. As she swung there she suddenly thought of the blue-shirt man and wished she had said thank you.

Sea Song

This is my place, my very own place,
Staring the ocean straight in the face.

Every morning I wake to find
The ocean in front and the hills behind.

Every morning I wake to see
The ocean carefully watching me.

I watch the ocean back again,
It stamps and whinnies and tosses its mane.

Bright and dangerous, bold and free,
Only a fool would trust the sea.

Mighty waters that call and move,
Only a fool could help but love.

Standing here I can know the sea,
But what in the world does it make of me?

Dreaming, dancing, false and true,
I can be bright and dangerous too.

Holding the hills and the sea and the sky,
A little reflection drowned in my eye.

The Princess
and the Clown

'Why are they ringing the bells?'

'Don't you know? The Princess is
marrying the clown today.'

'A princess marrying a clown? Are you
sure? Princesses don't marry clowns. They
marry princes, singers and seventh sons;
they marry the youngest of three brothers,
but not clowns.'

'No, I am quite sure this princess is
marrying a clown, a tumbling patchwork
fellow with a painted smile who falls flat on
his face when he bows. If someone stands

on his toe, water squirts out of his hat. This might be embarrassing at a State ball where everyone's toes get trodden on, but the Princess is going to marry him just the same.'

'Well, is this a *plain* princess?'

'No, she is beautiful, this Princess, a bit like a birthday cake and a bit like moonlight. She is warm and glowing like the birthday cake, and yet she is silvery like moonlight. She is like the first rocket going up, and spilling its stars on Guy Fawkes night - you know, when it is not quite dark and somebody can't wait so they set this first rocket off. It climbs so high it can see over the edge of the world and it calls to the sun, 'Look at me, brother!' Then it hesitates and opens up like a rose of flame, dropping petals of fire. That is the most magical rocket of all and the Princess is like that, or like the unicorn, rare and only. Anyhow, she is beautiful.'

'Why is she marrying a clown then?'

'It's a long story because lots of princes,

dazzling in gold and diamonds, came and asked her, "Princess, will you marry me?" And a lot of wise men with clever answers came to ask the same question. Hundreds of youngest sons appeared from all walks of life and asked the Princess if she'd marry them, but she always said, "Not today, thank you", to them all.

'This made them very angry and they got together and wondered how to pay her back for refusing to marry any of them.

'One day they went to her father, the King, and told him they had just the husband for her, and her father, the King, said, "Righto - we'll see him at dinner then, when pudding's over, just before we have coffee."

'The heralds all blew on their trumpets when the pudding plates were being carried away, and in came the clown. He did not know he was supposed to be asking for the Princess. He thought he was there to dance his dances and to make people laugh. This was a trick of the suitors to tease the clown and mock the Princess. The clown bowed to the King and the Princess and began to dance. He danced like a piece of crumpled wastepaper in the wind, twirling high and pettering low, and everyone laughed at him except the Princess who looked at him with grey eyes, gentle and calm.

'The clown trod on his own toe and water squirted out of the top of his hat. His smile was wide and painted on, and his red wig waved wildly in the air like a sort of lion's mane.

'He took out a little violin, the size of a toothbrush and began to play. Music as sweet as honeysuckle twined into the air, but as he played so beautifully his trousers slid down showing red striped underpants and knobbly knees. Everyone laughed and laughed but the Princess rested her chin on her hands and watched more closely. He danced his desolate little wastepaper dance again and played his violin while he spun and peeped, but people only laughed all the harder, for his coat split down the back and fell around him in coloured tatters like autumn rags. Then at last he bowed to the King, and as he did so he fell flat on his face – that clown.

'The King got to his feet. He was laughing

and angry at the same time. "You!" he shouted. "How dare you ask to marry my daughter!"

'The clown looked amazed. He did not know what the jealous suitors had told the King.

'But the Princess got up from her chair. "Dear Clown," she said, "I love you and will marry you if you like."

'"In that coat?" asked someone.

'"In it or out of it," said the Princess. "At least life would never be dull with a clown in the family."

'"Princess," said the clown, "you mustn't marry me. I make people laugh but I am not a cheerful person to live with. I'm really pretty sad." He took out a large red handkerchief, quite as big as a dishcloth and wiped off his paint and powder face. Off came his smile, his black eyebrows, his scarlet cheeks. Off came his red wig. The face of an ordinary man looked out at the world – young, a bit scared, rather sad and quite usual.

'Everyone laughed all over again.

'"Well," said the Princess, "when I'm sad you can make me laugh, and when you're sad I will try and make you laugh. That's fair, isn't it – but mind you, don't be cross with me if I'm not very good to begin with, because princesses aren't meant to make people laugh."

'"Well, personally," said the King, "I'm glad she's made up her mind at last. You shall marry this fine clown, my dear, if that is what you want, and maybe I'll get a laugh or two between the two of you whenever I come to visit. A laugh or two would spice even your cooking, my dear."

'The suitors did not even smile any more after that, but the King, who guessed their trick, laughed louder and louder.

'So the Princess is to marry the Clown and they will live part of the year in his caravan.

Their lives will be full of shadows and sunshine like night and day and they will parade like kings or dance like wastepaper – whatever they feel like – and probably live happily ever after.

'Let off all the fireworks, and blow up all the balloons, ring all the bells, blow all the trumpets . . . a princess is marrying a clown and they will have children half kings and queens, half tumble-down clowns, who will lead us through the twisted ways of the world with laughter.'

Margaret Mahy

WAIT FOR ME!

In this magical collection of stories by one of
the great writers for children there is a recipe
for a most unusual chocolate porridge; a goat
gives a surprise present to a little girl; a small
boy gets the better of the school bully; and
much more happens besides.

First published as *The Second Margaret Mahy
Storybook.*

'vivid, life-affirming stories ... A fine collection
from a master storyteller.'   *Dorset Daily Echo*

'A magical collection.'   *Family Interest
Magazine*

'The Mahy trademarks of joyous exuberance,
word play, unexpected twists, sheer fun and
playfulness are all there. Children who are
lucky enough to have this book read to them
will receive far more than just the story. They
will come to appreciate the power and
fascination of words.'   *Armadillo*

Also by Margaret Mahy

WONDERFUL ME!

Witches, mermaids, dragons, a boy who plays the violin and a girl who finds a dinosaur egg – all these and more appear in this book of stories and poems by one of the great writers of children's books.

Wonderful Me! was originally published as *The First Margaret Mahy Storybook* and these much-loved stories have appeared in many anthologies. As fresh and new as when they were first written, they are perfect to read aloud.

'Written with warmth and a gentle humour ... rich in surprises and imaginative twists.'
Family Interest